AS THE CITY SLEEPS

Stephen T. Johnson

VIKING

For Sophia and Emma

VIKING
Published by the Penguin Group
Penguin Putnam Books for Young Readers, 345 Hudson Street, New York, New York 10014, U.S.A.
Penguin Books Ltd, 80 Strand, London WC2R ORL, England
Penguin Books Australia Ltd, Ringwood, Victoria, Australia
Penguin Books Canada Ltd, 10 Alcorn Avenue, Toronto, Ontario, Canada M4V 3B2
Penguin Books (N.Z.) Ltd, 182-190 Wairau Road, Auckland 10, New Zealand

Penguin Books Ltd, Registered Offices: Harmondsworth, Middlesex, England

First published in 2002 by Viking, a division of Penguin Putnam Books for Young Readers.

1   3   5   7   9   10   8   6   4   2

LIBRARY OF CONGRESS CATALOGING-IN-PUBLICATION DATA
Johnson, Stephen, date-
As the city sleeps / by Stephen T. Johnson.
p. cm.
Summary: A look at the city at night reveals that innocent objects are not quite what
they seem once the sun has set.
ISBN 0-670-88940-7
[1. Night—Fiction. 2. City and town life—Fiction.] I. Title.
PZ7.J6373 As 2002 [Fic]—dc21   2002006166

Printed in Hong Kong
Set in Garamond No.3

Night, the beloved.

Night, when words fade and things come alive.

Antoine de Saint-Exupéry

Primal Return

They escaped into the night.

THE LEAVES

There was no wind.

THE NOISE WAS DEAFENING

Suddenly a defunct factory came alive.

A PECULIAR PAINTING

The frame could not contain its inhabitants.

FORSAKEN

Every night, the light appeared.

BROADWAY DREAMS

The lure of the lights was irresistible.

DRIVERLESS

The cab meandered through old haunts.

A Wondrous Find

From a simple stone came an unearthly glow.

GHOST RIDERS

Last seen in 1936, they vanished without a trace.

THE FOG

As it lingered by the ancient cathedral, singing began.

STRANGE PETS

Out for some fresh air.

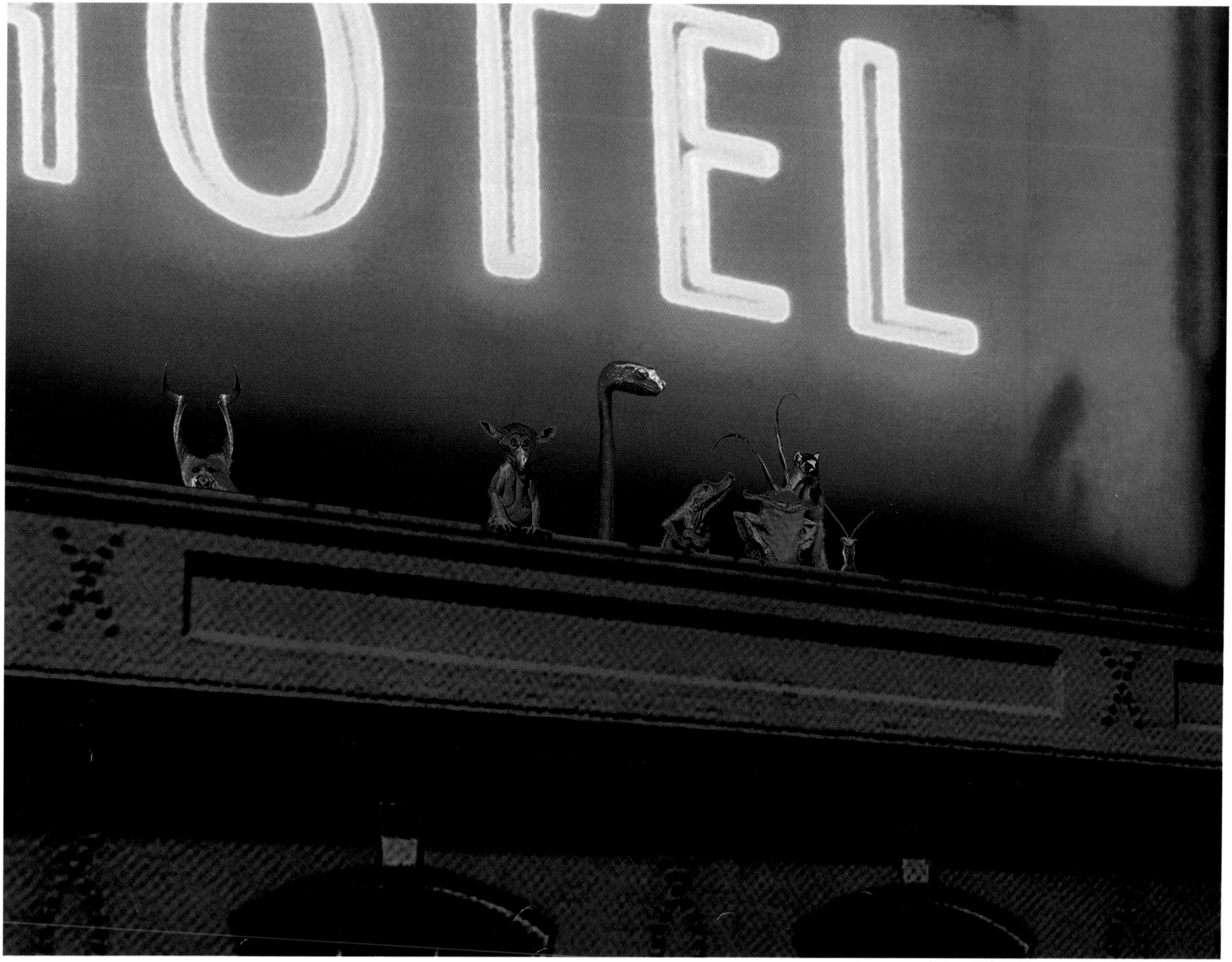
OTEL

NIGHT WINGS

Without a sound, it glided over the city.

APPARITION

Destination unknown.

TIME FOR BED

Even night creatures must sleep.